STAR WARS

The Empire Strikes Back Storybook

Based on the film *The Empire Strikes Back*
screenplay by Leigh Brackett and Lawrence Kasdan
story by George Lucas

Art Director/Editor	Eleanor Ehrhardt
Associate Designer	Roberta Pressel
Production Director	Edward McGill
Production Supervisor	Elaine Silber
Editor, Lucasfilm, Ltd.	Lindsay Smith
Storybook adaptation	Shep Steneman

Copyright © 1980 by Lucasfilm, Ltd. All rights reserved under International and Pan-American Copyright Conventions. Published in the United States by Random House, Inc., New York, and simultaneously in Canada by Random House of Canada Limited, Toronto.

Library of Congress Cataloging in Publication Data
Main entry under title:
The Empire strikes back storybook.
  Sequel to The Star Wars storybook.
  SUMMARY: The further adventures of Luke Skywalker and his friends in their continuing battle against Darth Vader and the evil side of the Force. [1. Science Fiction] I. Lucas, George. II. Steneman, Shep. III. Empire strikes back. [Motion picture]
PZ7.E696   [Fic]   79-5463
ISBN 0-394-84414-9 (trade)   ISBN 0-394-94414-3 (lib. bdg.)

Manufactured in the United States of America   1 2 3 4 5 6 7 8 9 0

TM Trademark owned by Lucasfilm, Ltd.

Princess Leia Organa
Leader in the Rebel Alliance

Chewbacca
A two-hundred-year-old
Wookiee, co-pilot of
the *Millennium Falcon*

Han Solo
Captain of the *Millennium Falcon*

Yoda
The Jedi Master, who
teaches Luke the ways of the Force

Luke Skywalker
Commander in the Rebel Alliance

Boba Fett
A notorious bounty
hunter of the galaxy

Darth Vader
The evil Imperial Lord, master
of the dark side of the Force

Lando Calrissian
The Administrator of Cloud City

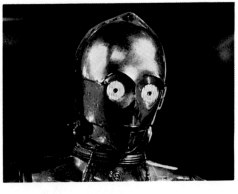

See-Threepio (C-3PO)
A tall, humanlike interpreter-droid

Artoo-Detoo (R2-D2)
A clever computer-repair robot

A long time ago in a galaxy far, far away, evil forces ruled with a terrible destructive power.

But the Rebel Alliance that had sprung up to oppose the Empire was growing stronger. The Rebels hoped to restore the high ideals and justice of the Old Republic.

Luke Skywalker, with the help of a mighty and mysterious Force, led the Rebellion to its greatest victory—the destruction of the Death Star, the Empire's most fearsome battle station.

But the war was far from over. The Empire was determined to crush the growing Rebellion. Imperial forces hunted the Rebels throughout the galaxy.

To escape the Empire's wrath, Princess Leia Organa and her band of freedom fighters secretly moved their headquarters to the bleak, frigid planet of Hoth.

As he rode his Tauntaun across Hoth's cold, lonely ice plain, Luke Skywalker dreamed of the warmth of Tatooine, his far-off home. Something dropping through the sky ahead suddenly jolted him back to reality. He reined his big snow lizard to a halt and focused his electrobinoculars.

"I think a meteorite just fell. I'm going to check it," he told Han Solo over his comlink. "Found any life readings?"

"Are you kidding?" Han's sarcastic voice crackled back. "There's not enough life on this ice cube to fill a star cruiser. See you at the base."

As Luke turned off his comlink, his Tauntaun reared in fright. "Whoa! I don't see anything out there, but I'll check again."

But before Luke could adjust his life-sensor, a shadow fell on him and he was terrified by a monstrous howl. Just as Luke turned around, a huge creature towered over him, and a big white claw swatted him from his mount.

Knocked unconscious, Luke never heard his Tauntaun's horrible death screams. He felt nothing as the monster dragged him across the ice. And he never discovered that the "meteorite" he'd spotted was really a strange dark robot that climbed out of the crater it had created and now floated across the ice plain.

The Rebel base was a series of ice caves. On the hangar deck, Chewbacca was welding a part on the *Millennium Falcon* when Han arrived back at the base. "How are you coming with those lifters?" he asked.

The Wookiee growled in reply.

"All right. I'll go report, and then I'll give you a hand. Soon as those lifters are fixed, we leave."

Han found Princess Leia and General Rieekan in the command center. "General," he said, "I think it's time for me to get along."

General Rieekan extended his hand. "You're good in a fight, Solo. I hate to lose you."

"Thanks, General, but you know about this price on my head. If I don't pay off that scoundrel Jabba the Hut, I'm a walking dead man. I should never have gotten involved with that smuggling operation." Han turned to Leia. "I guess this is it, Your Highness."

Leia gave him a frosty look. "I thought you had decided to stay."

"There's nothing I can do about it, Princess. Until I pay off Jabba, more and more bounty hunters will be searching for me. So long, Your Highness." Han left the room and started walking through the corridor.

Leia caught up with him. "We still need you. Don't you even care if . . ."

"Spare me! Don't tell me about the Rebellion again! Right now I've got my own head to think about."

"Sometimes I wonder if you even have one," Leia said angrily. "Enjoy your trip, hot shot!"

Leia and Han walked off in opposite directions. They never noticed the large white claw that broke through the ice wall behind them.

Luke Skywalker awoke to find himself a human stalactite hanging upside down from the jagged ceiling of an ice gorge. As he pulled himself up and tried to unfasten the thongs that bound his ankles, he heard his captor's chilling moan in the distance.

"Relax," Luke told himself. But when he spotted his lightsaber on the floor, a few feet out of reach, he couldn't take his own advice. He tried desperately to reach the sword, but it was no use.

Luke heard the ice monster's feet crunching toward him. Then he heard something else. Faint, almost a whisper, it was the voice of his old friend Ben Kenobi. "Luke, concentrate. Think the saber into your hand."

Luke stared at the saber, then squeezed his eyes shut in concentration. "Let the Force flow, Luke," said Ben's calm voice.

Luke flowed with the Force. Just as the ice monster loomed over him, the lightsaber jumped three feet into his hand. Quickly he ignited the sword and cut himself loose.

Then the ice creature was upon him. Luke scrambled to his feet and swung his lightsaber. The monster howled with pain and fell dead. Luke staggered away, wondering if he could keep from freezing in the frigid Hoth night.

On the base, a medical droid examined a dead Tauntaun. Han Solo joined a crowd of onlookers. "What happened?" he asked. "What killed it?"

"Neck broken," an officer told him.

"By what?" Han demanded.

"Unknown as yet," replied the droid.

Just then See-Threepio and Artoo-Detoo hurried in. "Master Solo, sir," Threepio said urgently, "Mistress Leia is looking for Master Luke."

"He's not back yet? It's almost night out there!" Han picked up his comlink and asked the deck officer if Luke had checked in yet. He hadn't.

Han turned toward a transport officer. "Are the speeders ready?"

"Not yet," the officer answered. "The night air is too cold. Maybe by morning."

"Then we'll have to go out on Tauntauns."

The officer shook his head. "The temperature is falling too rapidly. There's a blizzard out there."

"You bet there is," snapped Han Solo. "And Luke's out in it." He climbed onto a Tauntaun, pulled back on the reins, and rode out into the ice plain's frigid dusk.

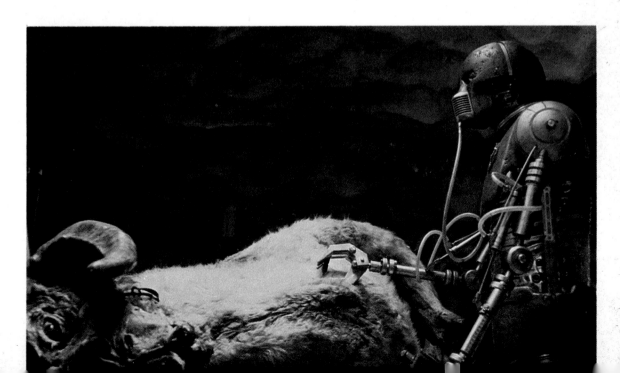

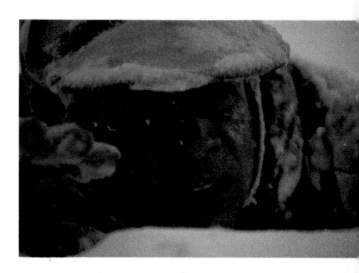

The howling wind knocked Luke Skywalker off his feet. He crawled a very short way, then collapsed. "I can't . . ." he cried feebly.

"You must," said the voice of Ben Kenobi.

Through the swirling snow, Luke saw old Ben standing near him. "You must survive, Luke. You must go to the Dagobah System. You will learn from Yoda, the Jedi Master who taught me. You're the Rebellion's only hope."

"Ben!" Luke cried, reaching toward him, but the image faded away. In its place Luke saw a Tauntaun and rider on the horizon. Then he collapsed, unconscious.

Han jumped from his lizard and cradled his friend in his arms. "Come on, buddy," he said, rubbing Luke's face. "Give me a sign. It's not your time yet."

Luke didn't respond. Han was desperate. He began to slap Luke. At last Luke gave a low groan. "I knew you wouldn't leave me out here all alone!" Han cried happily. He picked Luke up and carried him toward the Tauntaun.

Suddenly the lizard bellowed and fell over. It had frozen to death. Quickly Han lit Luke's saber, slit the Tauntaun's belly, and gutted the beast. He stuffed Luke inside the steaming carcass to protect him against the cold. Then he grabbed his comlink. It didn't work.

The blizzard was getting worse. Han pulled his supplies from the dead beast's back and struggled to set up a shelter. "If I don't get this up fast," he muttered to himself, "Jabba won't need those bounty hunters."

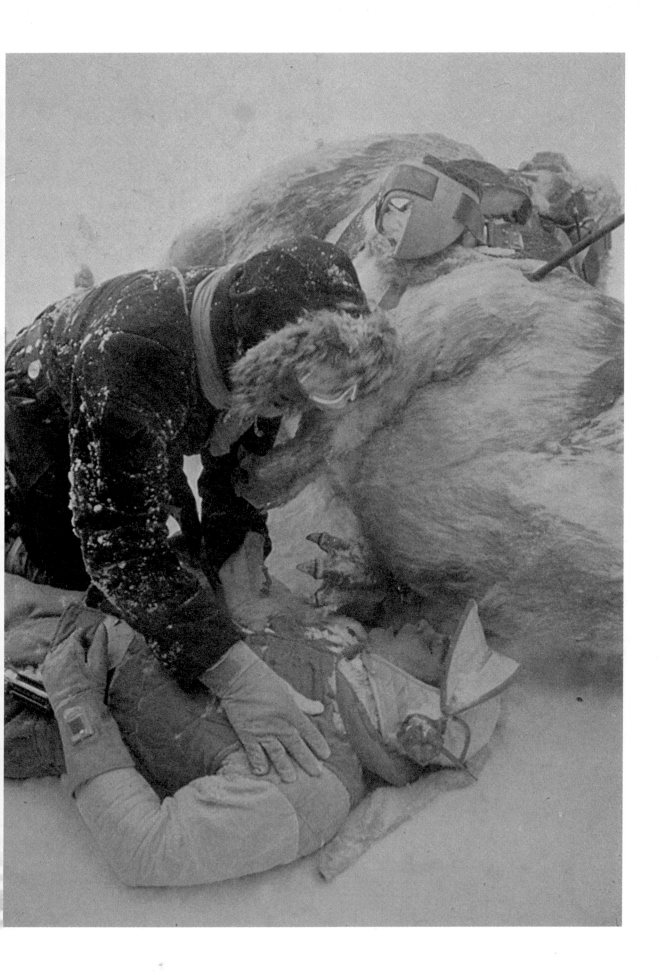

The next morning was cold and dim on the icy plain of Hoth as Leia, Chewbacca, Threepio, and Artoo anxiously watched a fleet of snowspeeders leave the base in search of Han and Luke. Moments later, a young pilot called Zev spotted a dim blip on his radar scope. "Echo three, this is Rogue two," he cried excitedly. "Do you copy?"

"Nice of you guys to drop by," squawked Han's voice over the static. "Hope we didn't get you up too early."

Zev swerved his speeder toward the signal. Outside his snow-covered shelter, Han waved frantically. The oncoming speeder was the most beautiful sight he'd seen in a very long time.

As his friends watched from an observation room, Luke thrashed about in the thick red slime of the base medical center's rejuvenation chamber. "Watch out!" he moaned as robot surgeons adjusted their equipment. "Snow creatures . . . dangerous . . . Yoda . . . only hope . . ."

"Doesn't make much sense," said Han.

"It would be most unfortunate," added Threepio, "if Master Luke were to develop a short circuit."

Han shook his head. "The kid ran into something mean, all right, and it wasn't just the cold."

"It was those creatures he keeps talking about," Leia said anxiously. "We've doubled the security, but . . ."

The surgeon droid's voice broke in. "Commander Skywalker is responding well. He will soon be out of danger." His friends let out a sigh of relief.

"Now we'd better find out what attacked him," said Leia.

When a few ice chips fell on Artoo-Detoo's head, the alert little robot stopped to investigate. Looking up, he discovered a crack in the ice wall of the corridor. Then Artoo saw two blinking eyes behind the crack. With an electronic yelp, he turned and ran.

Just in time! The wall behind him suddenly burst apart. Chunks of ice, steam, and frightening bellowing sounds filled the air. Troopers rushed to the scene, firing wildly at the monstrous form coming through the wall. One of the largest guns finally brought the creature down. As it fell, the corridor became strangely silent.

In seconds, alarms buzzed in every corner of the base, signaling full alert. "That creature didn't come through any of the checkpoints," General Rieekan told Leia and Han in the command center. Suddenly a wailing alarm screamed above all the others. He rushed to the console.

An officer pointed to a blip on a radar screen. Rieekan nodded glumly. "Princess, we have a visitor. In zone twelve, moving east. Something metal."

Leia looked puzzled. "Then it's not another one of those creatures."

"No. Wait, we're getting another signal."

Threepio listened intently. "I must say, sir, I am fluent in over six million forms of communication, but this is something new."

A voice on the communicator interrupted him. "This is Echo three-eight. Unidentified object in our scope. We should have visual contact in about . . ." The transmission went dead in a burst of static.

"Whatever it is, it isn't friendly," said Han Solo. "Come on, Chewie, let's have a look."

On the ice plain, the strange dark droid saw the speeder that was carrying Han and Chewbacca race toward it, with several others close behind. Instantly the robot extended an antenna and sent out a piercing electronic signal.

The lead speeder disappeared behind a nearby snowbank. A moment later, Chewbacca popped his head over the top.

The hostile droid turned toward him and aimed its deadly laser ray. But before it could shoot, Han blasted the robot from behind. It exploded into bits.

"There's not much left," Han reported over his comlink. "It's a droid of some kind. I didn't hit it that hard. It must have had a self-destruct."

Leia knew what that meant. She was sure it was an Imperial probe robot.

In another part of the galaxy, a convoy of Imperial Star Destroyers and TIE fighters roared through space with Darth Vader's ship in the lead.

"I think we've found something," young Captain Piett excitedly told his superiors. "The report we have is only a fragment, from a probe droid on Hoth, but it's the best lead on the Rebels in . . ."

Admiral Ozzel angrily interrupted him. "We have thousands of probe droids searching the galaxy, Captain. I want proof, not leads."

Darth Vader strode up. "Did you say Hoth, Captain?"

"Yes, sir," Piett replied nervously. "We have visuals. That system's supposed to be devoid of human forms, but . . ." He pointed to a huge screen.

Vader stared at the image. The tiny snowspeeders in the picture convinced him. "That's it."

"Lord Vader, there are many uncharted settlements," Admiral Ozzel advised. "It could be smugglers."

"That is the one!" Vader snapped. "Skywalker is there! Set your course for Hoth!"

Luke Skywalker lay on a bed in the medical center. "Master Luke, it's good to see you functional again," said Threepio. Artoo chirped in agreement.

"You're recovering well," Leia told him. "The scars should be gone in a day or two."

Luke touched her cheek anxiously. There was something he had to tell her. "Leia, what would you think if I went away for a while?"

Leia was startled. "Luke, where are *you* going?"

"To another system," Luke said quietly. "Not far."

Leia was furious. "I could get more loyalty if I recruited some of those ice creatures down the hall!"

"Ice creatures?"

"Oh yes, sir," Threepio replied. "They're being trapped quite cleverly. We discovered they are attracted to high-pitched sounds." Artoo-Detoo whistled to demonstrate.

Then Han and Chewbacca strode in. "Kid, you look strong enough to wrestle a Gundark," said Solo with all his usual cockiness. "That's two you owe me."

But before Luke had a chance to thank him, alarms began to scream. The sensors had detected a fleet of Imperial ships closing in on the planet of Hoth.

"An energy field is protecting our target," reported General Veers to Vader. "The shield is strong enough to deflect any bombardment."

Darth Vader clenched his fist. "Now the Rebels are alerted to our presence. That clumsy fool Ozzel came out of light-speed too close to the system. Prepare your troops for a surface attack."

As Veers departed, Vader activated a viewscreen. "Captain Piett!" he shouted.

As Piett stepped forward, he noticed Admiral Ozzel suddenly wheezing and panting for air.

"Make ready to land troops beyond the energy shield," Vader ordered. "Spread out our fleet so nothing can get off that planet. You're in command now, *Admiral* Piett."

Piett brightened at this news of his sudden promotion. But a moment later he was horrified. Beside him, Admiral Ozzel gasped, choked, and fell to the floor, dead.

Alarms sounded full alert as the Rebel forces prepared to defend themselves against the Imperials. Transport ships were prepared to evacuate the Rebels. On the hangar deck, Luke said a fond farewell to Han and Chewie, then rushed to his snowspeeder. Princess Leia and General Rieekan waited tensely in the command center as the first of the Rebel transports took off.

"One-three-zero approaching energy shield," said the controller. "Prepare to open shield."

With Imperial Star Destroyers hovering over it, the shield protecting the command center could be opened only for the briefest instant. As the first transport ships slipped through, a huge Rebel cannon fired powerful blasts to protect it. The power bolts slammed into an Imperial Destroyer. It spun out of control and the Rebel transport escaped.

Outside the base, Rebel troops worked feverishly to prepare their defense. Then above the howling wind, they began to hear a distant thump, thump, thump. Tiny dots on the horizon seemed to be inching nearer. The ground began to vibrate. The high-pitched rattle got louder. The Imperial Snow Walkers—huge, terrifying four-legged machines of destruction—were heading for the Rebel base.

Luke zoomed his speeder toward one of the machines. His tailgunner blasted away at it, but the fire just bounced away harmlessly. The Walker's armor was too strong for the speeder's weapons. As the monstrous machine fired back, Luke's little craft rocked in a hail of fire.

"Use your harpoons and cables!" Luke commanded his squadrons. "Go for the legs! It's our only chance!"

Across the plain, Luke's friend Wedge fired a harpoon across a Walker's front leg. He swung his speeder in and out among the machine's other legs, tangling them in the cable.

The giant Imperial assault machine began to stumble. Rebel troops in the trenches cheered as they watched it topple to the ground and explode.

Zev moved in on another Walker, but laser bolts turned his speeder into a ball of fire. Moments later Luke's craft was hit. It burst into flame and crashed.

An Imperial Walker was bearing down on him. There wasn't time for Luke to pull his tailgunner out of the wreckage. He grabbed a land mine and a gun and jumped. An instant later, the Walker's huge foot crushed his speeder flat.

Luke ran underneath the monstrous machine, fired a magnetic cable at its metal belly, and hoisted himself up with his utility belt. Hang-

ing right under the Walker, he cut a hatch open with his lightsaber. Then he tossed the land mine into the Walker and slid down the cable.

The blast stopped the Walker dead in its tracks. Nothing was left but a hollow shell. Behind it, Luke Skywalker lay unconscious from his fall.

After taking heavy fire, the Rebel base was a shambles. Pipes spewed steam; walls cracked apart; ceilings collapsed. As loudspeakers ordered the troops to evacuate, Han Solo ran into the command center to find Leia and Threepio. "You've got to get to your ship," Han told the Princess.

Suddenly a block of ice dropped from the ceiling and blocked their way. Han radioed the waiting transport ship. "We're cut off. You'll have to take off without the Princess."

He turned to Leia. "If we're lucky, we can still make it to the *Millennium Falcon*."

Outside, the Rebel troops began retreating. The forces of the Empire showed them no mercy. The Walkers pressed forward, their laser fire bombarding the Rebel position. "I have reached the power generators, Lord Vader," General Veers reported from his Walker. "The energy shield will be destroyed in moments."

But just then Veers saw a wounded speeder hurtling straight toward him. It crashed through the Walker's front window, blowing up the control panels in a blinding flash. The headless Walker toppled over on its side, useless.

Luke recovered just in time to see it happen. Still dazed, he trudged off through the snow and devastation toward the distant ice formation where his X-wing fighter awaited him.

Chewbacca let out a happy shriek. Han, Leia, and Threepio had made it to the *Millennium Falcon*. Dodging huge chunks of falling ice, they scrambled aboard.

In the cockpit, Han flipped some switches. Chewie barked a warning and pointed to a wobbling needle that might mean trouble.

"Would it help if I got out and pushed?" Leia asked sarcastically.

"Don't worry, Your Holiness," Han assured her. "This baby's still got a few surprises left in her."

A laser blast hit the side window. Han and Leia saw a squad of Imperial stormtroopers rush into the hangar. Han fired the *Falcon*'s cannons and pulled back on the throttle. "We'll just have to hope for the best," he said as the engines roared into action. "Punch it!" he cried to Chewie, and the *Falcon* rose into the sky.

Darth Vader watched it in disgust. "I want that ship," he told Admiral Piett, and he had no intention of being disappointed.

As he climbed aboard his X-wing fighter, Luke watched the *Millennium Falcon* streak past overhead. "At least Han got away," he said to himself.

An excited whistle greeted him. "Hello, Artoo," Luke said, settling into the cockpit. "Activate the power and stop worrying."

Han Solo had his hands full. Six swift TIE fighters and a huge Imperial Star Destroyer were right on the *Falcon*'s tail. Chewbacca howled a warning.

"Oh boy," Han muttered. "Two more Star Destroyers heading right at us."

"I'm glad you said there was no problem, or I'd be worried," Leia remarked.

Han scowled. "Chewie, how's the deflector shield holding up?"

The Wookiee barked a reply.

"Good," Han said confidently. "At sub-light, they may be faster, but we can still outmaneuver them. Hold on!"

He put the *Falcon* into a steep dive. Four TIE fighters followed him as he headed toward two oncoming Destroyers.

"That slowed them down a bit," he said. "Chewie, stand by to make the jump to light-speed."

"Those fighters are getting close," Leia told him.

"Yeah?" Han had a confident gleam in his eye. "Watch this!" He yanked the light-speed throttle. Absolutely nothing happened.

"Watch what?" Leia demanded. Han and Chewie looked at each other in amazement.

Han pulled the throttle again. Still nothing happened. "I think we're in trouble," he muttered.

Threepio spoke up. "Sir, I noticed earlier that the entire main para-light system seems to be damaged."

Chewie moaned. Han saw half a dozen TIE fighters narrowing the gap behind him. "We are in trouble," he admitted.

Aboard Luke's X-wing fighter, Artoo-Detoo sensed that something strange was happening. He beeped a puzzled question.

"There's nothing wrong, Artoo," Luke told him. "I'm just setting a new course."

Artoo sent up a long whistle of protest and concern. Luke read a translation on the computer scope. "We're going to the Dagobah System," Luke replied.

The little robot whirred in amazement. "Yes, I know it's against our orders. And I know it doesn't appear on our navigational charts. But don't worry, it's there. No, I'm not sure why we're going there."

Artoo beeped harshly. "I'm fine, Artoo," Luke replied calmly. "No dizziness, no drowsiness. We'll get there safely."

Artoo sighed.

Luke smiled at his worried friend.

The *Millennium Falcon* was steadily losing its race with the TIE fighters. In the hold, Han and Chewbacca worked frantically to make repairs.

Suddenly there was a loud thump against the *Falcon*'s side, and the ship lurched wildly. "That was no laser blast," Han said. "Something hit us!" He rushed to the cockpit.

"Asteroid!" Leia cried, pointing ahead.

Han pulled on the controls and dodged a chunk of rock. "Chewie, set two-seven-one."

"You're not seriously going into an asteroid field!" Leia exclaimed.

Han shrugged. "They won't follow us through this, so hang on. We're going to do some flying!"

Han steered his ship directly into the rock storm. Bobbing and weaving, the *Falcon* dodged the larger asteroids. The TIE fighters were close behind.

Chewie barked in terror as a small rock bounced off the ship. Threepio covered his eyes with his hands and prepared for the worst. Unwilling to show how frightened she really was, Leia sat staring straight ahead.

"We can't stay out here much longer," Han announced. "I'm taking us closer to one of those big ones."

"Closer!" cried Threepio and Leia in amazement and fright. Chewbacca barked in agreement.

The *Falcon* streaked past a giant asteroid, but two TIE fighters stayed right on its tail. Han dived just in time to avoid a huge, fast-moving chunk of rock. It tumbled across the TIE fighters' path, and the fighters disappeared in flames.

Then Han took his ship still lower, flying it into a huge crater. Slowing the craft, he spotted a small cave on the crater's far side and set a course for it.

Artoo and Luke stared at the gloomy cloud-covered planet below them. "That's Dagobah, Artoo. Looks a little grim, doesn't it?"

Artoo whimpered. "No, I don't want to change my mind," Luke said. "The sensors show strong life-form readings down there."

Artoo beeped worriedly. "Take it easy," Luke told him. "I'm sure it's perfectly safe for droids."

Luke took the fighter down through the clouds. Suddenly alarms began to shriek. Artoo whistled frantically. "All the scopes are dead!" Luke cried. "I can't see à thing. I'm going to start the landing cycle. Let's just hope there's something underneath us!" He threw a switch, and the retro-rockets fired with a deafening roar.

Moments later, the spacecraft landed with a terrible jolt. Luke opened his canopy and looked around. All he could see through the dense fog were some huge gnarled trees in a marshy bog. Then he heard a splash. Artoo had fallen overboard and disappeared.

As Luke jumped down into the water, a small periscope appeared and started to move toward shore. Artoo surfaced, let out a woeful whine, and disappeared again as a swamp creature took him under. Then a few bubbles appeared and WHOOOSH! Artoo was spit out of the water. He landed in a patch of moss with a series of electronic complaints and a case of injured pride.

The fog grew thicker. Sinister shadows and unfriendly eyes moved among the trees. Luke shivered with cold. "This seems like a bad dream. How are we going to get that ship flying again? What are we doing here?" A squirt of muddy water from one of Artoo's vent ports was his only answer.

Luke found a clearing, and set up camp. "Now I have to look for this Yoda. Seems like a strange place to find a Jedi Master, but there's something familiar about it. I feel like . . ."

"You feel like what?" asked a strange little voice. Luke grabbed his lightsaber and whirled around. Standing before him was a very odd creature about two feet tall.

"I feel like we're being watched," Luke replied.

"Away put your weapon," said the little fellow. "I mean no harm."

Luke hesitated, then lowered his saber. "Why are you here?" the small one asked him.

"I'm looking for someone," Luke replied cautiously.

"You've found someone, think I. Help you I can."

Luke tried hard to keep from smiling. "I don't think so. I'm looking for a great warrior."

"Not many of those," said the little one as he scampered into Luke's supply case. "Wars don't make anyone great." He grabbed Luke's tiny power lamp.

"Give me that," said Luke, growing impatient.

"Mine! Mine! Or I'll help you not!"

Artoo tried to wrestle the lamp away, but he wasn't quick enough. "I will help you find your friend," the wizened stranger told the irritated Luke.

"I'm not looking for a friend. I'm looking for a Jedi Master."

"Yoda you seek. Yoda!"

Luke was astonished. "You know him?"

"Of course, yes. I'll take you to him. But now eat we must. Come, come."

Luke hesitated—then, instructing Artoo to guard the camp, he followed the power lamp through the fog to a peculiar little clay house. It was so low inside that his head brushed the ceiling even when he was sitting down. "I told you, I'm not hungry," he protested as his host scurried about, fixing a meal. "Why can't we go see Yoda now?"

"Be patient. Soon you will see him. Why wish you to become a Jedi?"

"Because of my father, I guess."

The small person set food on the table. "Oh, your father. A powerful Jedi was he, powerful Jedi."

"How could you know my father?" Luke demanded. "You don't even know who I am."

Insulted, Luke's host turned away and spoke to someone else, someone Luke couldn't see. "No good is this. I cannot teach him. The boy has no patience."

"He will learn patience," replied the voice of Ben Kenobi.

"Much anger is in him. Like his father."

"We've discussed this before," said Ben's voice.

Luke realized now who the little fellow was. He could only be Yoda,

the Jedi Master. "I'm ready for my training," Luke said eagerly.

Yoda gave him a contemptuous stare. "What know you of ready? I have trained Jedi for eight hundred years. To become a Jedi takes the deepest commitment, the most serious mind."

"He can do it," said Ben's voice firmly.

Yoda turned toward the voice. "This one have I watched a long time. All his life he looked away to the sky, the horizon, the future. Never his mind on where he was, on what he was doing. Adventure, excitement

. . . a Jedi craves not these things." Yoda stared at Luke accusingly.

The young Rebel knew Yoda was right. "I have followed my feelings," he said, bowing his head.

"He will learn," Ben insisted.

"He is too old. Too set in his ways to start the training. And will he finish what he begins?"

"We've come this far," said Ben. "He is our only hope."

"I won't fail you," Luke declared. "I'm not afraid."

Yoda turned toward him with a glint in his eye. "You will be, young one. You will be."

Alone in his chamber, Darth Vader heard a commanding sound and made a low bow. A hologram of the Galactic Emperor appeared before him.

The Emperor's face was hidden in a dark, hooded robe. He spoke in a deep, rumbling voice even more fearsome than Vader's. "Our situation is most precarious. There is a great disturbance in the Force. We have a new enemy who could bring about our destruction."

"Our destruction? Who?" asked the Dark Lord.

"The son of Skywalker. The Force is strong with him. He must be destroyed."

"If he were one of us," Vader suggested, "he would be a powerful ally."

The Emperor considered Vader's words. "Yes," he finally agreed. "Can it be done?"

Vader dropped to his knees. "Emperor, he will join us or die."

Yoda began to teach Luke the ways of the Jedi. The training seemed beyond human endurance. Luke Skywalker had never felt so exhausted in his life.

With Yoda riding on his back, Luke had to run farther and faster than he'd believed possible. There was no time to rest. One test followed another. "Swing," cried Yoda, as he threw a small silver bar in front of Luke. He lit his lightsaber and swung at it, but it fell to the ground untouched. Luke fell, too.

"I can't," he gasped. "Too tired."

"Were you a Jedi, you could have cut it into seven pieces."

"I thought I was in good shape," Luke panted.

"But by what standard, ask I? Forget your old measures. Unlearn, unlearn!"

Luke had much to unlearn. Yoda began to lecture him on the ways of the Jedi. Time after time, Luke attempted Yoda's trials, and time after time he failed them. But with each new challenge, he could leap higher, run farther, and react faster. Yet he knew he was still a very long way from becoming a full-fledged Jedi Knight.

As Luke was standing on his hands one day, with Yoda jumping on his feet trying to knock him off balance, Artoo rushed up, whistling and beeping urgently. It broke Luke's concentration, and he collapsed. "What is it, Artoo?" he asked with annoyance.

Chirping madly, Artoo led Luke to the edge of the bog. The X-wing fighter had sunk in to its very tip. "Oh no," Luke moaned. "We'll never get it out now!"

Yoda stamped his foot. "Sure are you? Tried have you? Always with you it can't be done."

"Master, moving small things is one matter. This is a little different."

Yoda almost lost his temper. "No! No different! The differences are in your mind. Throw them out!"

Luke closed his eyes. "Okay. I'll give it a try."

"No," Yoda told him calmly. "Try not. *Do*. Or do not. There is no try."

Luke squeezed his eyelids shut and concentrated on thinking the ship out. The water began to boil and bubble. The fighter's nose began to rise. Then it slipped back and disappeared completely. "I can't," Luke said in frustration. "It's too big."

"Size has no meaning. It matters not. Judge me by size do you?"

Luke shook his head.

"And well you shouldn't. For my ally is the Force. A powerful ally it is. Life creates it and makes it grow. Its energy surrounds us."

The Jedi swept his arm in a vast circle. "Feel it you must. Feel the flow. Feel the Force around you. Here between us and there between that tree and that rock. Everywhere, waiting to be felt and used. Even between this land and that ship!"

The swamp began to burble. The nose of the fighter broke through the surface of the water. Grandly, majestically, the craft rose entirely out of the water and hovered above the swamp. Then, under Yoda's guidance, the X-wing moved like a graceful bird and touched down softly on the shore.

Luke was absolutely dumbfounded. When he finally found his voice, he could only stammer. "Master . . . I . . . I don't believe it."

Yoda stared him in the face. "That is why you fail."

After they landed in the cave, the *Falcon*'s crew worked long and hard at repairing the ship. Han and Chewbacca were making some final adjustments when Leia rushed into the hold. "There's something out there!" she cried. "I saw a slimy foot in the window. And eyes."

There was a sharp banging against the ship's hull. "I'm going out to see what it is," Han declared. "We just got this bucket going again, and I'm not about to let some varmint tear it apart." He grabbed a breath mask and tossed one to Chewbacca.

"You may need some help," Leia said, and picked up a mask.

"But that leaves me here all alone!" Threepio protested.

In the dark, dank atmosphere outside, Chewie spotted a leathery creature crawling across the top of the ship. Han blasted it with a laser bolt. The winged shape fell at the Princess's feet. "Looks like some kind of Mynock," she said.

Han nodded disgustedly. "There'll be more. They always travel in groups. They like nothing better than to attach themselves to ships. Just what we need right now."

Leia stamped her feet on the ground. "The ground of this asteroid cave is not like rock at all!"

Han knelt and studied the earth. He peered toward the mouth of the cave. "There's an awful lot of moisture in here," he agreed, and fired his blaster at the cave's far side. In a few seconds the ground began to buckle. "I was afraid of that," he said. "On board! Hurry!"

On their way up the platform, Han and the others had to cover their faces as two leather-winged Mynocks flapped past. Chewbacca slammed the main hatch shut. The ship began to heave and shake. "Fire her up!" Han told the Wookiee.

"The Imperial ships will spot us," Leia protested, trying to keep her balance in the rocking ship. "I know you can't jump to light-speed in this asteroid field."

Han pulled back on the throttle. "Strap yourself in, sweetheart! We're taking off!"

The ship strained forward. Barking, Chewbacca pointed ahead at rows of sharp, jagged stalactites and stalagmites that surrounded the entrance of the cave. More frightening yet, instead of seeming to grow bigger as the ship approached, the opening appeared to be getting smaller.

"The cave is collapsing!" Leia cried.

"This is no cave!" shouted Han Solo. "It's some kind of creature!"

Leia suddenly saw what he meant. The "stalactites" ahead were not rock formations at all. They were giant teeth!

"Bank, Chewie!" Han hollered. The *Falcon* rolled on its side and narrowly slipped between two of the creature's teeth. As the ship flew out into the asteroid field, the enormous jaws of a monstrous wormlike creature slammed shut behind it.

Aboard his Star Destroyer, Darth Vader was making absolutely certain the *Millennium Falcon* would be captured. He had called in the galaxy's most notorious bounty hunters: Bossk, Zuckuss, Dengar, IG-88, and Boba Fett, the most feared killer of them all.

"There will be a substantial reward for the one who finds the *Falcon*," Vader told them. "You may use any methods necessary."

Proud of his own forces, Admiral Piett looked at these soldiers of fortune with nothing but disgust. If the latest report from the Star Destroyer *Avenger* was true, these contemptible creatures would not be needed. "We have them!" Piett told Darth Vader.

"I can see the edge of the asteroid field," Threepio said as the *Falcon* narrowly missed an oncoming chunk of rock.

"Good," replied Solo. "Soon as we're clear, we'll kick into hyperdrive." But as the asteroids began to thin out, a bolt from the Imperial Star Destroyer *Avenger* blasted the *Falcon*'s tail.

"Stand by for light-speed. This time *they* get the surprise!" Han pulled back on the hyperdrive throttle.

Nothing happened. "This isn't fair!" Han cried as explosions from the *Avenger* burst all around. He tried again.

Nothing. "Sir, we've lost the rear deflector shield," Threepio reported. "One more direct hit on the back quarter, and we're done for."

"Sharp bank, Chewie," Han ordered. "Let's turn this bucket around!"

Chewbacca barked his disbelief. "You mean you're going to attack them?" Leia cried.

Han didn't waste his breath replying. He swung the ship around and aimed it toward the *Avenger*. Zigging and zagging to avoid enemy fire, the *Falcon* zoomed across the Imperial ship and shot directly toward the bridge.

The Imperial commanders couldn't believe their eyes. "He's insane!" cried Captain Needa. "We're going to collide!" But at the last instant, the *Falcon* veered off and vanished.

"Track them!" Needa ordered.

"The ship has disappeared from our scopes," an officer reported. "There's no trace of them."

"Scan the area once more," Captain Needa commanded. "I am responsible for this. When we rendezvous with Lord Vader, I will have to apologize to him myself."

Yoda calmly chewed on his three-pronged Gimer Stick as Luke Skywalker lay motionless in the muddy bog. Artoo prodded Luke awake. Rubbing his aching shoulder, the young apprentice glowered at two luminous balls hovering over his head. "I thought the seekers were set for stun," he complained. "They're a lot stronger than I expected."

"That would matter not were the Force flowing through you. Higher you'd jump! Faster you'd move! Open yourself to the Force you must!"

Luke lit his lightsaber and jumped to his feet. "I'm open to it now!" he said defiantly. "Come on!"

The glowing balls flew to Yoda's head. "This will not do. Anger is what you feel. Anger, fear, aggression—the dark side of the Force. Easily *they* flow. Beware, beware, beware of them. A heavy price is paid for the power they bring."

Luke lowered his saber. "Price? What do you mean?"

"The dark side beckons. If you start down the dark path, forever will it dominate your destiny. Consume you it will, as it did Obi-Wan's apprentice."

Luke nodded. "Vader. Then is the dark side stronger?"

"No, no. Easier. Quicker. More seductive."

"How am I to know the good side from the bad?"

"You will know. When you are at peace. Calm. A Jedi uses the Force for knowledge and defense. Never for attack."

"But why . . ."

Yoda cut him off. "There is no why. Clear your mind of questions. Quiet now. Be . . . at peace. . . ." Yoda's voice trailed off.

Luke closed his eyes and relaxed. Then he sensed the two glowing balls racing toward him. As they began firing stun bolts, Luke sprang to life, leaping every which way, deflecting bolts from all directions.

The balls suddenly retreated. "Much progress do you make, young one," said Yoda calmly as the seekers hovered above his head. "Stronger do you grow."

Luke grinned smugly. Then two more glowing spheres floated up from behind Yoda's back to join the first two. Luke's smile melted away.

"The *Millennium Falcon* definitely went into light-speed," Captain Needa told Darth Vader. "It is probably on the other side of the galaxy by now. I tried my best."

An instant later, Needa lay dead at the furious Dark Lord's feet. "Alert all commands," Vader ordered Admiral Piett. "Deploy the full fleet to search for that ship. And don't fail me, Admiral. I've had quite enough."

"Yes, Lord Vader," Piett replied, trying to conceal his terror. "We will find them."

Clinging to the side of the *Avenger*, the *Millennium Falcon* was dark, its power circuits shut down to avoid detection. "You could at least have warned Threepio before you turned him off!" Leia told Han indignantly.

"You think braking and shutting down in that amount of time is easy?"

"Okay, hot shot. What's your next move?"

Han pointed out the window. "The fleet's breaking up. I'm hoping they'll follow standard Imperial procedure and dump their garbage before they go into light-speed."

Leia smiled. "Not bad. Then what?"

"Then we have to find a safe port around here." He looked at a map on his computer screen. "Funny, I have the feeling I've been in this area before. Let me check." He focused an image on the screen. "I knew it. Lando! This should be interesting."

"Lando? Never heard of that system."

"It's not a system. He's a man. Lando Calrissian. Gambler, con artist, and all-around scoundrel. Runs a gas mine on Bespin. We go way back together."

"Can you trust him?"

"No. But he has absolutely no love for the Empire."

Chewbacca's bark broke in over the intercom. "Okay, Chewie. Prepare the manual release." Han grasped a lever. "Here goes nothing!"

As the *Avenger* jettisoned its junk, the *Falcon* tumbled along amid the debris. Han and Leia watched the Star Destroyer rev up its engines and disappear into hyperspace. Then Han started up the *Falcon*.

His plan had worked almost perfectly. Almost. Off in the distance, silently tracking the *Falcon*, was the ship of the bounty hunter Boba Fett.

Yoda rode on Luke's neck as he bounded through the bog with superhuman leaps. The little Jedi tossed a silver bar high in the air behind his apprentice. With one swift movement, Luke whirled, lit his saber, and cut the bar into four pieces. "Better," said Yoda. "The Force is with you."

But suddenly Luke felt a different sort of Force. "Something's not right," he said warily. "I feel danger . . . death." Turning, he saw a hulking black tree with twisted roots that framed a dark, sinister cave. Luke set Yoda down, and stared at the tree.

"It is strong with the dark side of the Force," Yoda said. "A servant of evil it is. Into it you must go."

"What's in there?" Luke asked.

"Only what you take with you."

Luke lit his saber, then moved toward the tree. "You won't need your weapon," Yoda warned, but Luke ignored him. The Master merely shrugged.

Hanging branches snapped at Luke, but he pushed past them and entered the cavelike opening in the tree. A smothering web fell on him but he cut through it with his sword. A beetle the size of his fist rushed up the wall beside him. Luke remained calm and walked deeper into the cave.

The cavern grew larger and became totally silent. Then Luke heard an abrupt hiss and saw a lightsaber flare up in the darkness. A shape appeared. Darth Vader seemed to be coming straight at him.

Luke slipped aside and swung his saber at the enemy. The Dark Lord's body disappeared into the darkness, but his helmet landed on the floor of the cave.

Then the helmet cracked and fell away. Luke gasped in terror at what he saw. It was an image of his own head! As the vision faded away, Luke slowly began to realize what it meant. He was not yet ready to face Darth Vader.

As the *Millennium Falcon* dived into the soft pink clouds of the planet Bespin, a twin-pod cloud car came up to intercept it. "Permission granted to land on Platform three-two-seven," the radio instructed. "Any deviation from your flight pattern will bring about your immediate destruction."

"I thought these people were friends of yours," Leia muttered.

"Well, it's been a while." Han took the ship down to the beautiful floating Cloud City. A motley collection of Bespin troops met them.

"I don't like this," Leia muttered.

"Wait here," Han said anxiously. "But keep your eyes open." He walked down the ramp with Chewbacca right behind him.

If Lando Calrissian was still Han's friend, he was doing his best to hide it. "Why, you slimy, double-crossing, no-good swindler—"

"I can explain everything, ol' buddy," Han interrupted, "if you'll only listen. . . ."

"I'll bet!" Lando laughed and gave his friend a hearty embrace. "Still wasting your time with this clown, Chewie?" he asked the Wookiee.

Then Leia came down the ramp. "Welcome," Lando said gallantly. "Who might you be?"

Leia introduced herself, and Lando kissed her hand. Han quickly steered him aside. "Lando, I don't intend to gamble her away. You may as well forget about her."

"That won't be easy, my friend. What brings you here, anyway?"

"Repairs."

Lando stopped in his tracks. "What have you done to my ship?" he moaned.

Han turned toward Leia. "Lando used to own the *Falcon*. Sometimes he forgets he lost her fair and square."

Lando nodded. "That ship saved my life more than a few times. I'll have my people get to work on her right away."

He led the group across the bridge to the center of the lovely Cloud City. Hearing some beeps and whistles, Threepio lagged behind. "An R2 unit!" he sighed wistfully. "I'd almost forgotten what they sound like." He walked through a doorway for a closer look.

Suddenly the door slammed shut behind him. "Oh my!" he cried. "I . . ." A laser blast cut him off and sent his arms, legs, and body flying in every direction. Bouncing off the walls, See-Threepio was little more than a bunch of spare parts.

On Dagobah, Luke was making steady progress. He could do a handstand on just one thumb. He could react faster than he'd imagined possible. And he could use the Force to lift objects as heavy as the amazed Artoo.

"Good, good," said Yoda, laughing for the first time. "Now be calm. Through the Force things you will see: places, thoughts, future, past, friends long gone."

Luke relaxed. "I see a city in the clouds."

"Bespin. Friends you have there, eh? Concentrate and see them you will."

"I see them!" Luke cried. "They're in pain!"

Yoda nodded. "It is the future you see."

Luke shuddered. "Will they die?"

"Difficult to see. Always in motion is the future."

"I've got to go to them," Luke said. "I've got to help them."

Yoda frowned. "Decide you must how to serve them best. If you leave now, help them you could. But you would destroy all for which they have fought and suffered."

Sensing Luke's gloom, Artoo tried to console him. But nothing could cheer the young apprentice who had such a terrible decision to make.

Han Solo was telling Leia how beautiful she looked in Cloud City's soft light when the door flew open and Chewbacca stormed in. With irritated barks he set a boxful of Threepio's parts on a table.

"He found him in a junk pile," Han translated.

Leia was outraged. "What a mess! Chewie, can you repair him?"

"Why don't we just let Lando's people do it?" Han asked.

"No," Leia said firmly. "Something's wrong here. Your friend's charming, but I don't trust him."

"Now, listen, sweetheart, I'm not going to have you accusing . . ."

Han didn't finish his sentence. Lando appeared at the door and invited his guests to dinner. Hungry as they were, they could hardly refuse the offer.

"Lando," Han asked on the way, "aren't you afraid the Empire might discover this operation and shut you down?"

"That's always been a danger," Lando admitted. "Much of our trade is . . . well, unofficial. But I've just made an arrangement that will keep the Empire out of here forever."

The doors to the dining hall slid open. At the far end of the long banquet table sat Darth Vader. Boba Fett stood right behind him.

"Sorry, friend, I had no choice. I told you I made an arrangement," Lando told Han. "They arrived right before you did."

"I'm sorry, too," said Han, drawing his blaster and firing at Vader. The Dark Lord raised his hand and the bolts bounced harmlessly into the walls. Then Han's weapon suddenly whisked across the room into the evil one's hand.

"We would be honored if you would join us," said Darth Vader.

"My friends are in trouble," Luke cried out, awakening from a fitful sleep.

"You must not go," Yoda said simply.

"If I don't, Han and Leia will die."

The shimmering image of Ben Kenobi answered him. "You don't know that. Even Yoda cannot see their fate."

"I can help them!" Luke protested.

"You're not ready yet. You still have much to learn," said Ben.

"The tree!" Yoda reminded Luke. "Remember your failure at the tree."

"I've learned much since then. And I'll return to finish my training. I promise that."

Ben's voice grew stern. "Luke, I will not lose you to the Emperor, as I lost Vader. Only a fully trained Jedi Knight, with the Force as his ally, will prevail. If you end your training now, if you choose the easy path—as Vader did—you will become an agent of evil. You are the last Jedi, Luke—our only hope. Be patient."

"And sacrifice Han and Leia?"

Yoda stood up. "If you honor what they fight for—yes!"

Luke grappled with the problem as long as he could bear it. Finally he made his decision.

"I cannot protect you," Ben reminded him as he prepared the X-wing fighter for takeoff. "If you choose to face Vader, you will do it alone. Once you've made the decision, I cannot interfere."

"I understand," said Luke.

"Use the Force only for knowledge and defense," Ben pleaded, "not as a weapon. Don't give in to hate, anger, fear. They lead the way to the dark side."

Luke nodded and climbed into the cockpit.

"Strong is Vader," Yoda told him. "Clouded is your future. Mind what you have learned. Notice everything —*everything!* It can save you."

"I will," said Luke. "And I'll be back. I give you my word."

Artoo closed the cockpit, and Luke took the ship up and away. "Told you I did," Yoda reminded Ben. "Reckless is he. Things will worsen."

"The boy is our last hope," Ben replied.

"No," answered Yoda as his keen eyes watched the X-wing ship disappear in the sky. "There is another."

Alone in a cell in Cloud City's prison, Chewbacca howled with frustration as he paced back and forth. His huge fists pounded the walls so hard the lights went out. Whimpering, he sat down on a cot with Threepio's disassembled parts. Picking up the torso, he stuck the head on top and fiddled with some circuits. Suddenly Threepio's eyes lit up, and he began to mumble. The Wookiee made some adjustments. "Watch out!" cried the golden droid. "There are Imperial troops all . . . Oh no!" he shrieked, noticing he was not all together. "I've been shot!"

Paying no attention to Threepio's jabber, Chewie kept on working. Soon he had an arm attached. "Something's still not right," Threepio insisted. "Why, my head's on backward! Only a flea-bitten mophead like you would . . ."

Chewie shut him down as two stormtroopers flung Han Solo into the cell. Hugging him, the Wookiee barked with worry. Han had been gone a long time, and he looked battered and bruised. "I'm all right," he said, exhausted.

Two more troopers tossed Leia into the cell. Overjoyed to find each other still alive, she and Han embraced warmly. "I can't understand what they're up to," Han told her. "They had me howling in that torture chamber, but they never asked me any questions."

Lando and two guards came through the door. "Get out of here!" Han shouted, standing up. "You fixed us all pretty good. Some friend!" he shouted, as he charged Lando and punched him hard. Lando fought back, and his guards quickly knocked Han away with their rifle butts.

"Look, I've done what I can for you," Lando said, rubbing his sore jaw. "Vader's agreed to turn Leia and Chewie over to me, but he's given you to the bounty hunter. Vader doesn't care about you at all. He's setting a trap for someone called Skywalker."

"And we're the bait!" Leia snapped bitterly as she went to tend Han's bloody chin.

A platform rose from a deep pit surrounded by pipes, hoses, and tubes of chemicals. Frightened but helpless, Lando stood by as Ugnaughts scurried around preparing the chamber.

"The facility is crude, but it should suit our needs," Darth Vader told Lando approvingly.

One of Vader's aides burst in with urgent news. "Ship approaching, sir. X-wing class."

"Good. Monitor Skywalker's progress and allow him to land. We'll have this chamber ready for him shortly."

Lando looked shaken. "We only use this facility for carbon freezing. If you put him in here, it might kill him."

"I don't wish the Emperor's prize to be damaged," Vader replied. "We will test it first. Bring in Solo."

Then Boba Fett and a squad of stormtroopers brought in Han, Leia, and Chewbacca. Threepio was strapped to the Wookiee's back, the robot's legs and one arm still unattached and dangling from a pack.

"Put Solo in the freezing chamber," Vader ordered.

"What if he doesn't survive?" Fett demanded. "He's worth a lot to me."

"The Empire will compensate you for your loss," said Vader. His troopers thrust Han toward the platform.

"No! No!" Leia cried. Chewie charged wildly at the stormtroopers. Within seconds, reinforcements arrived and handcuffed the furious Wookiee.

Chewbacca barked a sad farewell to Han. "I know," his friend replied, choking with emotion. "I feel the same way."

Leia took Han in her arms. "I love you," she said, her eyes filling with tears. "I wish I'd told you before."

Han tried to be brave. "Remember that, 'cause I'll be back." He kissed her softly on the forehead.

Tears rolled down Leia's cheeks as she watched Han walk to the platform. Lando winced as the Ugnaughts bound his friend's arms and legs. Chewie moaned desolately as Han turned to take one last look at his friends. Then the platform dropped into the pit. Leia turned away in agony.

With a shower of sparks, fiery molten liquid poured into the pit. "They're encasing him in carbonite," Threepio explained. "It's a high-quality alloy, much better than my own. He should be quite well protected . . . if he survives the freezing process."

Big mechanical tongs lifted a thick metal block from the pit and stood it on the platform. Ugnaughts rushed over and slid the block into a coffin-like capsule. Lando checked some readouts and exhaled with relief. "He's alive. In perfect hibernation."

"All yours, bounty hunter," Vader told Fett.

"I'll take the others now," said Lando.

"Prepare the chamber for our new arrival," Vader ordered. "Then you may take these others. But I'm keeping troops here to watch over them."

"That wasn't the bargain," Lando protested. "You said the Empire wouldn't interfere in . . ."

Vader cut him off. "I'm altering the bargain. Just pray I don't alter it further."

Luke found Bespin uncommonly welcoming. No patrol ships came to intercept his fighter as he approached Cloud City. And no one displayed the slightest hostility as he and Artoo searched for their friends. It all seemed extremely odd.

Luke remained on his guard. When he heard voices coming toward him in a deserted corridor, he ducked into a doorway with Artoo.

Pushing Han's encased body between them, two guards followed Boba Fett around a corner. The instant he spotted Luke, Fett drew his gun and shot at him, but the Jedi apprentice dodged away and fired back. Fett raced down a passageway and by the time Luke reached it, a thick metal door had sealed it off.

"Leia!" Luke shouted as he saw stormtroopers lead her across the corridor with Chewbacca and Threepio.

"Luke, no!" Leia cried as she and the others went through a doorway. "It's a trap!"

Without thinking, Luke tore after her. Suddenly he found himself in a tall, cylindrical room with hissing pipes and a platform in the center—it was the carbon-freezing chamber. As Luke searched for his friends, a giant metal door clanged down and cut him off from Artoo. Then more doors slammed shut. There was only one exit left: an opening in the ceiling. Suddenly the platform he was standing on rose toward it.

The huge room above was silent and empty. Luke cautiously moved toward a stairway. Gradually he sensed something evil nearby.

"Lord Vader," he called, looking for his enemy. "I feel your presence. Show yourself. Or do you fear me?"

All at once the room filled with steam. Through it, Luke could make out a dark figure on a walkway overhead. Confidently, Luke started up the stairs. "The Force is with you," he heard Darth Vader say, "but you are not a Jedi yet."

Reaching the walkway, Luke lit his sword. Vader ignited his saber. Luke lunged at him and missed. He slashed out again, but Vader drove him back. Yet Luke still felt he was in command. Again and again he rushed at Vader, and again and again Vader retreated.

"The fear does not reach you," said the Dark Lord. "You have learned more than I expected."

"I'm full of surprises," replied the young Rebel.

"And I, too." With spectacular speed, Vader sent Luke's saber flying out of his hand. Then he struck at Luke's feet.

Luke tumbled down the stairs to the deck below. He looked up to see Vader, like a giant black bird, flying straight down at him. Luke rolled away from the Dark Lord.

"Your future lies with me," said Vader, circling. "Now you will embrace the dark side."

"No!" Luke cried defiantly as he backed away.

"There is much Obi-Wan didn't tell you. Come, I shall complete your training."

"I'll die first," said Luke.

"That won't be necessary." Vader suddenly charged forward, knocking Luke back into the open pit. "Too easy," Vader mused as freezing steam rose from it. "Perhaps you are not as strong as the Emperor thought."

Behind Vader, something streaked up from the pit just before molten metal poured down into it. "Time will tell," Luke said, hanging from some hoses above the Dark Lord's head. Yoda's lessons in leaping had served his apprentice well.

"Your agility is impressive," said Vader. Luke jumped down to the platform and raised his hand. His lightsaber jumped from across the pit into his outstretched hand and lit up.

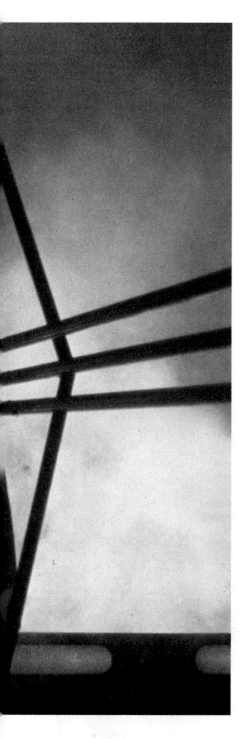

Vader circled nearer. "Ben has taught you well. You have controlled your fear. Now release your anger. I destroyed your family. Take your revenge!"

Lightsabers clashed, and Luke drove Vader back. "Your hatred can give you the power to destroy me!" Vader taunted. "Use it!"

"I will not become a slave to the dark side," Luke told himself. Swinging his sword, he sent Vader falling into the pit.

Luke went to the edge and looked down, but his enemy was nowhere to be seen. Reminding himself to be cautious, Luke slowly lowered himself into the pit.

The fierce Imperial stormtroopers marched Leia, Lando, Chewbacca, and Threepio down a corridor. They came to an intersection guarded by Lando's men.

"Code Force seven," Lando commanded without hesitation, and his guards instantly aimed their weapons at the surprised troopers.

"Hold them in the security tower," Lando ordered. He took two of the stormtroopers' guns and handed one to Leia. "We're getting out of here," he told her as he released Chewbacca's bindings. But when the Wookiee's hands were freed, he put them around Lando's neck.

"After what you did to Han," Leia told him, "I wouldn't trust you to . . ."

"I had no choice," Lando gasped, trying to free himself from Chewbacca's choking grip. "There's still a chance to save him. They're at the East Platform."

Leia's eyes brightened. "Chewie, let go! We've got to hurry!"

Artoo-Detoo saw them rush by. Beeping wildly, the little droid scooted after them. He was delighted to see his old friends again, even if Threepio didn't seem quite himself.

When they arrived at the landing platform, Leia went limp. Boba Fett's ship had taken off and was zooming toward the sunset. Chewbacca howled and fired at it, but the craft carrying Han's body was already out of range.

A bolt of laser fire exploded next to Leia. "Move!" Lando shouted, hurrying to the elevator with Artoo. But the frustrated Leia and Chewbacca stood their ground, firing blast after blast at the oncoming stormtroopers.

"Artoo, help me!" Threepio cried as laser fire crackled all around him. "It's a fate worse than death to be strapped to a Wookiee!"

As the troopers closed in, Leia and Chewie backed into the elevator. The door slammed shut just in time.

Luke climbed down to the lower level of the freezing chamber. Vader stood motionless in the control room. "Attack," said the Dark Lord without igniting his saber. "Only by taking revenge can you save yourself."

Confused, Luke hesitated. Then, as he raised his sword with both hands, a huge piece of machinery came crashing toward him from behind. Luke whirled and cut it in half, and then the whole room seemed to come alive. Machines hurtled toward him, pipes and sparking wires whipped at him, but he used the Force to turn them aside. Although he summoned up every ounce of energy he had left, small tools and parts stung him, leaving him bloody and bruised. A fierce wind began to howl, swirling everything around.

Vader stood unmoving in the center of it all. "You are beaten. It is useless to resist."

Luke knew he was losing the battle. As he felt the Force weaken within him, a huge chunk of metal knocked him out the window and into the reactor room.

Luke clung to the edge of the platform and looked down into the bottomless space below him. As he scrambled up to safety, loudspeakers everywhere commanded Vader's forces to seal off the city. "Your friends will never escape, and neither will you," Vader declared.

Luke lit his saber and made a vicious lunge. The shoulder of Vader's armor smoked and sparked, and the Dark Lord put his hand to the spot. "Don't let yourself be destroyed as Obi-Wan did," he thundered.

"Calm, be calm," Luke told himself. Then Darth Vader charged toward him.

Wind began to howl in the reactor shaft as Luke and Vader clashed swords. Suddenly, Vader slashed an instrument panel apart. As Luke glanced at it floating away in the wind, Darth Vader's saber slashed his arm. Wincing with pain, Luke dropped his sword and backed away.

"There is no escape," Vader said, moving closer. "Don't make me destroy you. You are strong with the Force. Now you must learn to use the dark side. Join me and together we shall be more powerful than the Emperor." •

He put down his sword and extended his hand. "Come, Luke," he continued. "I will complete your training and we will rule the galaxy together."

"No! I will never join you." Luke drew back to the edge of the platform.

Vader stepped forward and spoke slowly. "If you only knew the power of the dark side. Obi-Wan never told you what happened to your father."

Luke glared at Vader. "He told me you killed him."

"No, Luke. I am your father."

Luke stared in horror at the Dark Lord. "No!" he gasped. "That's not true. That's impossible!"

Again Vader moved forward. "Search your feelings. You know it is true. Luke, you can destroy the Emperor. You can have everything you could ever want. It is your destiny. Join me and we can rule the galaxy as father and son. Come with me. It is the only way."

But there was another way. It was the only way for Luke. With the utmost calm, Luke stepped off the platform and let himself fall into the chasm.

Vader rushed forward and made Luke a witness to the Dark Lord's power. He held out his hand and a great wind caught hold of Luke. It swept him back up the shaft. Then Vader gestured again and, as abruptly as it had started, the wind ceased. Vader let him go. Now Luke was falling again—faster and faster.

Suddenly he was being pulled toward an exhaust pipe—and he was sucked into it.

Luke clung to the edge of the exhaust pipe with every last bit of his strength. It wasn't enough.

As he slid out of the pipe, he grabbed desperately at Cloud City's weather vane. To his astonishment, the delicate instrument supported his weight. "Ben!" he pleaded as he climbed onto the vane. "Ben!" But the Jedi Knight did not appear.

Luke turned his appeal in another direction. He had felt his friends' pain and suffering across the galaxy. Now he hoped they might sense his call. "Leia," he murmured as a piece of the weather vane snapped off. "Leia, hear me."

As Chewbacca held off a group of stormtroopers at the *Falcon*'s docking platform, Lando ordered his citizens to evacuate the planet. Leia tried to open the door leading to the ship, but it wouldn't budge. Imperial forces had programmed it shut.

Lando and his friends held off their attackers while Artoo tried to open the door to another platform. A special series of beeps was the key. The exit flew open. "Artoo, I knew you could do it!" Threepio cried happily.

Everyone scrambled aboard the *Falcon*. Chewie and the droids fired up the engine. Leia and Lando took the controls, and the ship climbed through the clouds.

Aboard the *Falcon*, Leia's face suddenly darkened with worry. "We've got to go back! Chewie, head for the bottom of the city."

"We can't go back there," Lando told her. "What about those TIE fighters on our tail?"

Leia gave him a harsh stare, and Chewbacca growled viciously.

"Okay, okay." Lando shrugged. "Try it."

Below, the city was in chaos. Desperate to leave, the residents had to haul their belongings and fight the Imperial troops at the same time.

The *Falcon* approached the underside of the city.

"Look!" cried Lando. "On the weather vane! It's Luke."

The three TIE fighters were closing in behind the *Falcon*.

"Fly as near to him as possible," Leia ordered Chewbacca. The skillful Wookiee piloted the ship perfectly. Then, as Leia and Chewie desperately fought off the enemy fire, Lando opened the top hatch and reached out to the battered warrior.

In an instant Lando grabbed Luke and pulled him into the *Falcon*.

"Lando, is he all right?" Leia called into the intercom. "Lando, do you hear me? How is Luke?"

"He'll survive," replied a very weary Luke Skywalker, wrapped in a blanket.

Leia ran to him and hugged him.

Alarms began buzzing on the control panel. Lando sat down in the pilot's chair. "The deflector shield is going," he said grimly. "And there's another ship, much bigger, trying to cut us off."

Luke looked beaten. "Vader," he murmured.

"We've got nothing to worry about," Lando told Leia. "If my men said they fixed this baby, they did."

"I hope you're right," said Leia as explosions tossed the ship around. "It's now or never."

"Punch it!" Lando cried.

Chewbacca pulled on the light-speed throttle. The engines whined faster and faster and—shut down.

Luke was shattered. He sensed Vader's ship coming nearer, and he was certain he had failed. He moaned the Dark Lord's name. "I won't be able to resist him."

Chewbacca rushed into the hold, where Artoo was busy putting Threepio together. "We're doomed!" Threepio groaned. Vader has deactivated the hyperdrive. And just when I'm nearly well!"

Artoo beeped an opinion. "Oh, Artoo, how would you know what's wrong?" Threepio scolded. "Mind my feet and stop your chattering."

Across the hold, Chewbacca pounded angrily at a panel that refused to function. Artoo couldn't wait a moment longer. He rushed to the wall, pulled out a circuit board, and turned one of its tiny parts around. Suddenly the ship tilted up and tossed him on top of Chewbacca. The engines began to scream.

"We did it!" cried Lando, tumbling from his chair. The *Millennium Falcon* shot into hyperspace and another part of the galaxy. Darth Vader seethed with helpless fury as he watched it disappear.

The *Falcon* docked with a Rebel cruiser—but not for long. Han Solo was still in mortal danger somewhere, and Lando and Chewbacca were anxious to find him. They said their good-byes and prepared the ship for takeoff.

With heroic Artoo and nearly new Threepio next to them, Luke and Leia watched the craft depart. The Princess was silently praying for Han's safe return. The Jedi apprentice was thinking about his unfinished training and the uncertain future.